Slates and Bowls

Kyuka Lilymjok

ISBN 978-978-969-223-1

Published by:
Free Pen Publishers
10 Lachlan Close, Maitama, Abuja

Any people depicted in stock imagery provided by Thinkstock are models, and such images are being used for such purposes only.

This book is printed on acid-free paper.

The views expressed in this work are solely those of the author and do not necessarily reflect the views of the publisher. The publisher hereby disclaims any responsibility for them.

To my Wife Maria and my children: Justice, Sunfair and Fairprincess

Holding the slate, Mujahid was always angry with his parents. He could kill them for bringing him into the world only to abandon him in a madrasa with a slate and on the streets with a bowl to fend for himself when he was not of age. If he could kill his parents, was it unbelievers and so-called Moslems he could not kill?

Chapter One

In one of the thrown-together neighbourhoods of Azeri lived Gazali a renowned Islamic scholar many Moslem children from far and near went to his madrasa to acquire Islamic literacy and knowledge. Gazali's house which doubled as his school composed of four separate buildings with a square courtyard at the centre of the buildings. In front of the house facing the road was a long veranda pupils who attended his school received their instructions. Each day, Gazali sat on a chair on the veranda of his house dishing out knowledge in spoonful to his pupils who surrounded him sitting on mats spread on the veranda.

About Gazali and his pupils, pigeons would be flying cooing to the open sky. To an unattending passerby, recitations by the pupils of what they were taught by their teacher when at a lower pitch sounded like the cooing of the pigeons also. To a biased passerby, the pupils not only sound like cooing pigeons, they had the brains of pigeons.

Mujahid was one of Gazali's committed and dutiful pupils. He attended to his lessons religiously with all the attention needed for understanding and recollecting what was taught. But Mujahid was waspish. There was always a wasp in his brain that could sting anyone any time. In addition, he had traces of radical Islam. Now and then flames of hate and contempt for infidels flared in his eyes when Islamic lessons or conversation with friends wound round *unbelievers*.

Mujahid shared his fanaticism with Gazali his teacher. Indeed, Gazali could be said to inspire Mujahid with his fanatical zeal which he graduated from Gazali's Madrasa with and later gave limb to with destructive consequences.

As a grownup, Mujahid was a short man who having to look up at others always made angry. He was also angry others were looking down at him. Slight in frame, he was angry others were occupying more space in life than he was. In a car he could not occupy much space. This also made him angry particularly if the car was his and he was sitting in it with someone bigger than him.

The average day for Mujahid in Gazali's Madrasa began as early as 4.30 am. He was usually woken up by the muezzin's call for the early morning prayers. When he enrolled as a pupil at the madrasa, the muezzin then calling the faithful to prayers had a musical way of performing his duty that thrilled him. Every word of the prayer ballad was distinctively pronounced with a lot of gusto while the words making a sentence in the ballad rolled into a song Mujahid found melodious.

Though not often expressed, many Moslems in Hausaland disdained the job of a muezzin. Because the job was not well regarded, there was a saying that it was a demeaning thing for the emir to call people to prayers while commoners strut about. There was no doubt Musa knew the low esteem his office suffered, but this fact did not seem to dampen his zeal for the job. It seemed to be his thinking that he could introduce colour into an otherwise drab job.

While pretending not to do so, Mujahid had listened to a conversation between Musa the muezzin and Gazali his teacher.

'You are good at your job,' Gazali said. 'I have been around for a long while; I can't remember any muezzin that does it as well as you do.'

'For me, it is a very important job,' Musa said. 'Prayers is the second and perhaps most important pillar of Islam after faith. Calling people to prayers therefore is a very important assignment.'

'You are right,' Gazali said. 'Calling people to prayers is calling them to Islam. So calling people to prayer can even be what will lead to faith.'

'You have said something there,' Musa said. 'Declaration of faith is the first pillar of Islam. But declaration of faith without prayers can easily make faith wither away. A muezzin calling the faithful to prayers is actually calling them to affirmation of faith and paradise.'

Unfortunately, Musa the muezzin died and was replaced by one who wasn't as enthusiastic for the job as his predecessor. Lacking interest for the job, the new muezzin seemed to be performing the task perfunctorily without the gusto and relish his predecessor performed it. He called the faithful to prayers with a certain languor in his voice that seemed to say if you like, come; if you don't like don't come. Sometime, he was even late calling for prayers. There was a day he slept off and the Imam had to make the prayer call himself. When reprimanded by the Imam, he said he was not paid for the job and so should not be harassed.

'As if I am paid to be Imam,' the Imam quipped.

'You may not be paid in cash, you are paid in regard,' the muezzin retorted. 'In addition to regard, now and then someone strays into your house and doles something out to you; what of me? No money, no regard.'

'I earnestly implore you to look at your assignment differently,' the Imam said. 'Calling people to prayers is calling them to salvation and there is nothing more rewarding than this.'

The admonitions of the Imam did not seem to have any significant impact on the muezzin as he continued to perform his duty without the desired zest and commitment. Despite the muezzin's lack of spark however, his call never failed to wake up Mujahid for the early morning prayers. Woken up, he proceeded to perform his ablution and headed to the nearby mosque.

At the mosque, he was always at the front row behind the Imam leading the prayers. He detested anyone being between him and the Imam. People between him and the Imam share his reward and he did not like this. Behind the Imam, reward flowed directly from God through the Imam to him.

Chapter Two

Teaching and learning at Gazali's madrasa began as soon as there was sufficient daylight for the pupils to write and read on their slates. This was usually around 6.30 in the morning. When teaching his pupils, Gazali never forgot to tell them to read only the Quran and no other book. When Allah commands Moslems in the Quran to read, he commands them to read only the Quran and not any kafir literature – pagan literature. Whenever he was reading the Quran, flames of fire leapt from the holy book into his eyes and from his eyes to his pupils. When reading the Quran, he said he could hear laughter in heaven and lamentations in hell.

A frequent subject in Gazali's madrasa was jihad. There was hardly a day in his teaching of his pupils that Gazali would not talk about jihad. 'There are three forms of jihad,' he had at the beginning of Mujahid's pupillage with him elaborated. 'The first form is jihad of the heart. This jihad is hating whatever is wrong or evil,' he said, flames of fire, which he called flames of piety, flaring in his eyes as they usually did whenever he was talking about jihad. 'This form of jihad is the weakest and womanish form of jihad,' he said with a tinge of contempt in his voice.

'Why is this form of jihad the weakest and womanish form of jihad?' Mujahid asked.

'Because there is nothing requiring courage or manliness in it,' Gazali said. 'Merely hating something in one's heart does not expose one to any danger. No one is privy to the thoughts in a man's heart. Only in the heart, this form of jihad does not purify or advance Islam much.'

'I see,' Mujahid said with deep understanding of what his teacher had said. 'Why is it the most widespread,' he asked.

'Because it is cheap,' Gazali said with unveiled contempt. 'Anything cheap is always everywhere. Grasses are cheap; they are everywhere. Diamonds are not cheap; they are rare to find.'

'I see,' Mujahid said.

'The second form of jihad is jihad of the mouth,' Gazali pontificated, the flames of piety in his eyes flaring higher. 'This form of jihad requires a believer to bring jihad of the heart to the mouth by speaking against what he hates in his heart; by speaking against evil.'

'I see,' Mujahid muttered.

'The worst evil this type of jihad speaks against is the evil of unbelief or that of pretending to believe.'

'Unbelief or pretending to believe,' one of the pupils murmured in a drawl.

Though it was only a murmur, Gazali heard it. His ears were very sharp. He often said his ears were so good that he could hear the terrible things happening in hell and that was why he was doing his best to avoid ending up there. 'I believe you have no problem understanding unbelief is refusing to believe in Islam, but may have problems understanding pretending to believe refers to so-called Moslems who pretend to believe in Islam, but in truth do not,' he went on in a rabid tone. 'In my mind, so-called Moslems are worse evil than outright infidels. You know an infidel when you see one. He does not pray with you and so can't stab you in the back. You don't so easily know a so-called Moslem when you see one. He prays with you and so can stab you in the back.'

'Hmm ...,' many of the pupils snorted nodding their heads at the same time.

'A so-called Moslem is a hypocrite and hypocrisy is one of the four awful sins in Islam alongside homosexuality, usury and apostasy,' Gazali continued, his face contorting into an ugly scowl as if expressing his resentment of the four awful sins. 'A hypocrite is a counterfeit, and a counterfeit is always worse than mud. Do you understand?' he asked all the pupils.

'We understand Mallam,' the pupils said.

'So-called Moslems – the hypocrites, are the enemies within that are more dangerous than the enemy without – the outright infidel. So-called Moslems should be fought more viciously than the outright infidel because they are more pernicious than infidels,' Gazali said with fervour.

'Very true Mallam,' the pupils chorused.

'Unbelief and pretending to believe are the worst form of evil because it is from them other evils spring,' Gazali continued with rabid intensity. 'Stealing, murder, adultery, drunkenness, theft, corruption of all kinds all flow from the fountain of unbelief or pretending to believe. There would have been no stealing, murder, adultery, drunkenness and other vices if there was no unbelief or hypocrisy of belief. You can imagine the idyllic world we would have been living in.'

'Woe to unbelief and hypocrisy of belief,' the pupils chorused.

'By saying what you just said, you are already waging the second form of jihad which is far better than the first form,' Gazali said smiling warmly at his pupils. 'Though better than the first type, the second type of jihad is only faintly manly. For the most part, it is loudly womanly,' he went on in a rabid tone.

'Why is it faintly manly and loudly womanly?' a pupil asked.

'Because words are not manly; they are womanly,'Gazali said rapidly. 'It is action that is manly and this is where the third form of jihad comes in.'

'The third form of jihad,' Mujahid enthused with passion.

'Yes, the third and last form of jihad,' Gazali echoed with zest. 'The third form of jihad takes jihad of the mouth to the hand. This form of jihad carries a flaming sword. If unbelievers and so-called Moslems would not listen to the mouth, they would listen to the hand with the sword. This is a manly and rarest form of jihad.'

'Why is it rarest?' a pupil asked.

'Because action is expensive and rare; because it commits the life and property of the jihadist to danger,' Gazali said. 'Human beings for the most part flee from what exposes their lives or property to harm. Do you understand?' he asked the usual way.

'We understand, Mallam,' the pupils chorused.

'Common to all forms of jihad is resentment of evil and hatred of what is not part of Allah. Without such resentment and hatred of evil, there is no faith in Islam. This means it is jihad that constitutes faith in Islam. This is why when jihad of the hand is about consuming an unbeliever but he recites *kalmatu shahada,*[*] he is spared death. Reciting *kalmatu shahada* means he resents and hates evil. Jihad is part of faith. No jihad, no faith; no faith, no Islam. Jihad and faith are two sides of the same coin: jihad constituting faith and faith invigorating jihad.

---

[*] Kalmatu Shahada is a declaration of faith in Islam that: There is only one God, and Mohammed is his messenger.

'If jihad constitutes faith, it means it is in the first pillar of Islam,' Gazali went on with a singular insight into his brand of Islam. Jihad is not only at the heart of the first pillar of Islam, it is its holiest part. It is the most sacred duty of a Moslem. Of course, you should know that other pillars of Islam are meaningless without the first pillar where jihad resides. Without the first pillar, other pillars hang on nothing.

'If the first form of Jihad is the weakest form of jihad, it is the weakest form of faith,' Gazali went on his voice rising to a fiery pitch. 'If the second form of Jihad is a fairly strong form of jihad, it is a fairly strong form of faith. If the last form of Jihad is the strongest form of jihad, it is the strongest form of faith.

'Jihad is the anger of Allah advancing on infidels and so-called Moslems,' he continued after a momentary pause. 'A jihadist is the courier of this anger. Jihad is not only the means by which Islam is advanced, it is the means by which Islam is purified. It is the most holy and pious activity in Islam.'

'Ahead of fasting?' a pupil asked.

'Ahead of fasting,' Gazali stammered, lowering his gaze.

'Islam means peace; how can peace be attained through jihad of the hand?' another pupil asked.

An ugly scowl crept into Gazali's face, but quickly disappeared. 'Peace will only be attained when everyone becomes a Moslem,' he said in a haunting tone. 'The world if you don't know is divided into two,' he continued after a momentary pause. 'The two parts the world is divided into is the abode of Islam and the abode of *kafir*. The abode of Islam is the abode of peace where all Moslems are. The abode of *kafir* is the abode of war where all infidels are. The abode of Islam is in perpetual war with the abode of kafir and that is why there can be no peace in the world. Peace will only come to the world when the abode of Islam has taken over the whole world and as far as I can see this will be very long in coming.'

As a pupil of a madrasa, there was no subject Mujahid liked listening to like jihad. Whenever Gazali was talking about jihad, he listened with rapt attention.

Chapter Three

Teaching and learning started early at Gazali's madrasa because the pupils would later have to go out to do menial jobs in town or work in Gazali's farm if it was rainy season or harvest period. The pupils fended for themselves and often for Gazali and his family as well. Fending for themselves, they went out to carry things for people mostly in wheelbarrows; cut people's fingernails; fetch water and wash clothes for people. They also begged for alms in the form of food or money. When they returned from their various enterprises for survival, they gave Gazali part of what they had eked. Paying no school fees, what they gave him was their school fees. When he felt he was not bleeding enough money from them, he took them to his farm to bleed labour out of them.

In town fending for himself, Mujahid begged for food or fetched water for a fee. Begging for food was mostly in the morning. When begging for food, he and other children either stood in front of a house begging in a sing-song to be given food or followed a little girl selling *Kosai* – bean cake, and pap.

In front of a house with their begging bowls, Mujahid and other almajiris[*] would in a sing-song be begging for any leftover of the previous night meal: *'Ko dan kanzo, ko dan tsaki tsaki, almajiri maraya[*].'* Slates had been left behind in the madrasa. Bowls were now where the slates were – in the hands of the *almajiris*.

If there was any food leftover in a house, it would be brought and poured into the begging bowls of the *almajiris*. On receiving the food, the *almajiris* if hungry, squatted down and devoured it in front of the house they were given the food. If they were not hungry they moved on with the food. It would be their lunch or even dinner. If after standing for a long time in front of a house, no one comes out to give them food or tell them there is no food, they moved on to the next house.

One day Mujahid and other *almajiris* were in front of a house begging for food when a lot of rice was brought to them from the house. Though

---

[*] Pupils from a madrasa
[*] A begging song sang by pupils from a madrasa calling on people in a house to give them the leftover or dregs of their meals.

they had always been given food in this house, what they were given this day was more than what they were used to. They were very hungry and immediately began eating the food with the ferocity of famished hyenas. From experience, this might be the only big food they would be given that morning. Haunted by this fear, each of them strove to hurl in as much of the rice as fast as he could. As they scooped the rice with their palms to their mouths, some of it fell to the ground through their fingers. Soon the bowl was empty, but the ground around them was littered with a lot of rice that fell from their hands while taking it to their mouths. Though each of them spilt the rice, it was clear Husaini a boy with a big head and big lips spilt more than others.

'Husaini, why are you always spilling more food than everyone?' Mujahid asked the boy angrily.

'And why should you be the one to query me?' Husaini retorted. 'Is it your father's rice?'

'You who is always spilling food, is it your father's food you always spill? Do you even have a father?' Mujahid spat.

'You who have a father, why are you on the street with the rest of us without fathers?' Husaini howled back at Mujahid.

For a while Mujahid could not say anything. He was always quick to call other children bastards or to insinuate this when he did not know his own father that much. The person he called his father he had not had much to do with him. How then did he develop this penchant of calling other children bastards when they may be better fathered than he was?

'Who is even your father?' a boy Mujahid had once called a bastard asked as if reading Mujahid's thoughts. 'At least my father and Husaini's father had once visited our school, but your father has never done so.'

Mujahid's heart lurched. What the boy said was true. While the other boys' fathers had visited their school, his so-called father had not. Was the man he called his father truly his father? His mother had questions to answer he fumed. 'My father is too busy and too far away to come to our school,' he said.

'Busy doing what?' Husaini sniggered.

'Busy doing your mother,' Mujahid retorted

'Your father is a pig; he can't do my mother,' Husaini said.

'Your mother is a dog, she ...'

At this point, an old woman from a nearby house leaned out of the house, her hand holding a dish apparently containing food she wanted to give the *almajiris*. They all forgot their quarrel and ran to her.

Mujahid was the first of the three boys to reach the old woman. So she emptied the food in her bowl into his bowl and went back into the house. The other children knowing Mujahid would not share the food with them, walked to the next house to try their luck.

There was a Hausa saying that *almajiri tsuntsu ne; in ya ci abinchi tashi zai yi* – the Quranic pupil is a bird, he will fly away as soon as he finished eating food. Because an almajiri will abandon his work once his stomach is full, people who give almajiri work do not give him food until he has done the work. As soon as the almajiris with Mujahid were given food in the house they went to, they hurried away from the house. Mujahid tailed them.

Some days, instead of going from house to house begging for leftover food, Mujahid and other almajiris followed little girls hawking kosai hoping someone would buy the *kosai* and share to them as *sadaka* – a popular form of alms in Hausaland. *Sadaka* is usually given by people seeking one favour or the other from God. Usually when these alms are given, the person giving the alms expects the *almajiris* to pray for him. Being innocent children who are virgins, their prayers are more likely to be answered than those of adults. In Azeri, it was a common thing to see a little girl hawking kosai in front of little boys trailing her. Whenever she came by someone who looked like he had money and would buy the *kosai*, she would walk to him and say, '*za ka saya*? – will you buy? If he bought, often he bought for the girl to share what he bought to the *almajiris* trailing her.

Chapter Four

Mujahid did not know his parents the way he knew the streets of Azeri. Though he had spent part of his childhood with his parents, he seemed not to know them much. When still with them in his hometown, he was more on the streets trying to eke a living than at home with them. Away from home for four years, his recollection of his parents was becoming vague and hazy.

His father Naziru had four wives and forty-eight children. He had some of these children with the four wives now with him and others with wives he had divorced. His children were so many he did not know the names of some of them. Beckoning Mujahid one day to send him on an errand, he asked him what his name was. Mujahid was shocked and angry at the same time. How could his father be asking him his name? He told him his name but did not run the errand. Instead of going to find out if his father's friend and neighbour was at home, he hung somewhere and later returned to tell his father the friend was not at home. When he was seven years old, there was an embarrassing tale of his father seeking to marry his daughter by one of the wives he had divorced. According to the story, his father met a girl in Noka and proposed marriage to her. The girl told her mother who she was living with about the proposal. The mother told her to invite home the man who proposed the marriage. The girl did so and Naziru turned up. The mother on seeing him started crying. Naziru on seeing her slumped his head on his chest in shame. He had proposed marriage to his own daughter.

Naziru was a messenger in the ministry of works and housing of his state. His salary of thirty thousand naira was not enough to feed five people and they were fifty three in the house. Every day, he and his siblings went out to work for what to eat or beg for it. All day they were out on the streets trying to eke a living.

Naziru liked eating *suya* – skewered meat, and drinking *shai* – tea. But because of the size of his family, he could not afford to buy skewered meat for the whole family or purchase tea provisions for it. So he always went out at night to buy skewered meat from *mai-suya – skewered meat seller*. After eating the meat, if he had more money, he was likely to also buy *shai* from *mai-shai* – tea seller. With his stomach full, he would return home. When given the food cooked at home which was always a very poor meal, he would say he was not hungry. One day he was at a *mai-shai* stall taking tea with fried eggs and bread when conversation sprung up between him and a man he had always met at the stall.

'Sometimes I feel bad when sitting here to drink tea knowing my family cannot drink it at home,' the man said.

'I used to feel so, but no longer,' Naziru said savouring the eggs he was eating. 'I can't provide tea for the many mouths in my house.'

'But how do you and I come by the many mouths in our houses?' the other man wondered aloud.

Naziru did not think the man expected him to reply him, so he said nothing. But a man sitting next to him replied the man who asked the question. 'The fact is that we are irresponsible people,' he said.

'Perhaps you are right,' Naziru said. 'But our irresponsibility has produced something good.'

'What good thing has it produced?' the man next to him asked in a voice laden with disdain.

'It has made Hausa people the first people in Jeddere to have a market, if not the first people in the whole of Africa to attain this feat,' Naziru said.

'I don't understand,' the man said.

'Not being able provide meat or tea for the household the way other tribes were, Hausa men who must eat meat and drink tea could only do so outside their homes. So *mai-suya* and *mai-shai* sprung up to provide these delicacies. Around these two, other sellers of commodities and services also sprung up. Today, there is hardly any small community in Hausaland that does not have a market.'

Mujahid came to Azeri when he was barely eight years old. He was brought to the town by his father who said he wanted him to acquire Quranic education. Since his father brought him four years ago, he had not gone home, neither had his father or mother bothered to come and see him.

In Azeri, Mujahid met Dan'azumi who said he was from Saugu. According to Dan'azumi, he came to Azeri without intending or knowing he was doing so. A day before the day he found himself in Azeri, he had gone out with other children begging for alms. When they were tired, they scrambled into the back of a lorry where he slept off. His friends later left the lorry without waking him. When he woke up, he was shocked to find it was not only night but that the lorry was in motion. He was afraid, but could not jump off the lorry while it was in motion, and at night. At least the lorry was taking him to a town. If he gets off the lorry, he might be doing so where he may come to harm. He was lucky he still had some food in his begging bowl. Resigning himself to fate, he ate the food in the bowl. He was sure the lorry driver did not know he was in the lorry. Sleeping curled up in the lorry as he usually did, the driver if he looked into the trunk of the lorry, must have in the darkness of the night he left Saugu mistaken him as one of the objects in the trunk of the lorry. Later he fell asleep again and only woke up when the lorry stopped at Azeri. As soon as the lorry stopped, he jumped down from it and landed as softly as he could, then slunk away into the town. For days, he wandered the streets of Azeri sleeping by their sides at night and waking up in the morning to trudge them. At night, there were always murmurs and whispers in the street he did not know where they were coming from. Yet, he was not unduly afraid. Neither was he unduly distressed because even in Saugu, his life was not particularly different. After two weeks in Azeri, he ended up in in Gazali's Madrasa where he met Mujahid.

Chapter Five

Four things defined Mujahid's life and indeed that of any almajiri – the slate, the bowl, begging and the street. At the madrasa, the slate was in hand and learning took place though it was often distracted from by thoughts of where the next meal would come from.

Holding the slate, Mujahid was always angry with unbelievers who he blamed for hunger, injustice and wayward behaviour he was seeing in the world. There would have been more food, less injustice and waywardness in the world if everyone was a Moslem. Hunger, injustice and wayward behaviour would have disappeared from the earth if Islam was the only religion in the world.

'I don't agree with you,' Dan'azumi said to him one day when as usual he blamed unbelievers for hunger, injustice and waywardness in the world. 'From what you told me, your father could not provide food for you and he is neither just nor responsible,' Dan'azumi said.

'You are right,' Mujahid said.

'Is your father not a Moslem?'

'He is.'

'So?'

'My father is a *so-so* Moslem; in fact, he is a *so-so* human being,' Mujahid said the wasp in his head flying about looking for who to sting. 'When I talk of the world being all Moslems, I don't mean my father's type of Moslem. I mean serious minded Moslems.'

'Unfortunately, most Moslems around the world are your father's and my father's type of Moslems,' Dan'azumi said and there is no hope if you convert the whole world to Islam, the same will not be the case. In fact, it could even be worse. Without other religions to make Moslems want to give dignity to their own in the hope of converting non-Moslems, Moslems would easily slip further into anomie and shameful behaviour.'

'I don't agree with you,' Mujahid said.

'I never said you should,' Dan'azumi said. 'I was only saying what I think.'

Holding the slate, Mujahid was always angry with his parents. He could kill them for bringing him into the world only to abandon him in a madrasa with a slate and on the streets with a bowl to fend for himself when he was not of age.

If he could kill his parents, was it unbelievers and so-called Moslems he could not kill?

As he insisted being on the front row in the mosque, Mujahid insisted being in the front row at the Madrasa. His slate appeared bigger than the slates of other pupils; so did his pen. Sitting in the front row, he heard what his teacher was saying more distinctively and without distraction except that of hunger. While listening to the teaching of Gazali or reciting the Quran after him, a chiming fervour was always branded on his face like the sword of Dindin.* Now and then the fervour turned light, then dark depending on whether he was excited or angered by what he was being taught. He was always excited when teaching was on heroic acts of Prophet Mohammed, his companions or successors, and angry when it was on those who refused to accept Islam. Strangely, he seemed to be indifferent to teachings on the pious acts of the prophet, his companions and successors.

He liked the booty and thunder Surahs of the Quran more than other Surahs. In the booty

* The sword of Didin was a sword that was branded on the followers of the Dindin religion as a symbol of chivalry.

Surah, he liked the verse that urged believers not to flee from unbelievers in battle and the one that says it is not believers that strike unbelievers in battle but Allah himself. He liked the thunder surah because he saw Allah as thunder. In battle, Allah was the thunder that strikes unbelievers. Out of battle, Allah was the flames of fire that scorched unbelievers who desecrated him with unbelief.

Unlike Mujahid who saw Allah as a fiery spirit being in constant war with unbelievers, Suleiman from Sufyan madrasa saw Allah differently. The Sufyan madrasa was run by Imam Sufyan who saw Islam as a religion of peace. In his teachings of his pupils, he talked of peace and progress flowing from Allah, not violence and war. Instead of barking at unbelievers through thunder, Allah the Supreme Being lovingly beckons to unbelievers to believe in him and do right by him and their fellow human beings.

Unlike Gazali who told his pupils Allah wanted them to read only the Quran, Sufyan told his pupils Allah wants them to read everything. According to him, it was by reading everything they would appreciate Islam better.

Mujahid and Suleiman often met in the course of their menial jobs in town to fend for themselves and their Mallams. One day when they met, Suleiman said if he grows up and makes money, he would buy a piece of cloth and sew a coat to which Mujahid quipped in Hausa, *'ka fito arnen ka ba*? – and come out your infidel, enh?'

Suleiman was shocked to silence by his friend's response to what he said. He was not only shocked by what his friend said, but the violence and contempt he said it. Looking into Mujahid's face, all he saw was contempt and hate for suits which he was pining for. As a child, he could not compose his thinking well on the matter. As he grew older, he started wondering why wearing suits should make him an infidel. No doubt, suits were commonly worn by Christians and other non-Moslems while gowns, long robes and regalia were commonly worn by Moslems. But why should these cultural preferences become part of religious faith? How does the type of clothes one wears affect his faith? Thinking about this, he wondered why as a Moslem, he could not be called Peter or Stephen. How does a name affect one's faith? Was faith supposed to be about clothes and names or about hearts and minds? Later, he found that Islam in Hausaland not only frowned at wearing certain kind of clothes and bearing certain types of names, it also disdained speaking in English language. In the market one day, a Hausa man was speaking Hausa to an Igbo man. The Igbo man who did not understand much Hausa replied the Hausa man in English. The Hausa man not understanding much English and seeing it as a signpost of unbelief, called on his son Kabiru who could speak English and therefore knew *kafirci* – heathenism, to come and *kafirce* – heathenize the Igbo man for him. When Kabiru came, he said to him in Hausa, '*kafirce man shi* – heathenize him for me.'

Instead of being angry, he laughed at the absurdity of what the Hausa man had said. Language was what it was – a means of communication. Why should speaking a particular language make one a heathen if he believed in God?

Chapter Six

Long after graduation from their madrasas, Mujahid and Suleiman both residing in Azeri, always met. Whenever they met, conversations between them never wandered far from their understanding of the Quran and the teachings of their Mallams.

'Whoever is not a Moslem is an infidel in the abode of war,' Mujahid said in one of their conversations.

'I hold a different opinion,' Suleiman said. 'My opinion is that Islam is one among other religions in the world. 'When we call people who don't believe in Islam infidels, they also call us infidels for not holding their own faith.'

'How dare them?' Mujahid spat violently.

'How dare you?' Suleiman retorted.

'Everyone is born a Moslem,' Mujahid barked

'So says Islam,' Suleiman said. 'No other religion says everyone is born a Moslem. Anyone can claim for himself what he thinks of himself.'

'Islam is a universal religion revealed for all mankind,' Mujahid said as if he had not heard what Suleiman said.

'Other religions also make similar claims for themselves,' Suleiman said. 'To attract followers, every religion claims to be the only way. If it says there are other ways, it is telling people they can follow those other faiths and still make heaven. Religions are monopolies and the God of almost every religion is a jealous God who does not want other Gods to compete with him for worshippers.'

'Are you sure, it was a madrasa you attended?' Mujahid asked Suleiman scarcely concealing his contempt for the latter.

'It was a madrasa I attended alright,' Suleiman said. 'The fundamental difference between my madrasa and yours is that yours sees the world only with the eyes of Islam while mine sees the world with the eyes of Islam and other religions.'

'Islam must prevail throughout the world,' Mujahid said as if he had not heard what Suleiman said. 'That's why the abode of Islam must be in perpetual war with the abode of unbelievers until they become Moslems. For now, what we have is not Islam but Jihad. It is when the abode of kafir has been swallowed by the abode of Islam, that you will have Islam.'

'But you said a while ago that everyone is born a Moslem,' Suleiman interposed. 'If everyone is born a Moslem, how do we come by the abode of peace inhabited by Moslems and the bode of war inhabited by non-Moslems?'

Something ugly appeared in Mujahid's eyes but quickly disappeared. 'True everyone is born a Moslem, but not everyone professes Islam,' he said. 'Even among Moslems professing Islam, not everyone is a true Moslem. There are many so-called Moslems. Moslems not professing Islam and Moslems professing Islam but are not true Moslems are those in the abode of *kafir* while true Moslems are those in the abode of Islam. The abode of Islam is in perpetual war with the abode of *kafir* until everyone becomes a Moslem and the whole world thereby becomes the abode of Islam.'

'How can there be peace in an abode of Islam that is in perpetual war with the abode of *kafir*?' Suleiman asked in a tone that sounded mocking to Mujahid. 'You know the common saying that a child that says its mother will not sleep, will also not sleep. How can Islam have peace if it is always at war?'

'The common saying you just referred to is a *kafir* saying unworthy of the mouth of a true Moslem,' Mujahid said, his voice thick with contempt and a murderous expression bestriding his face.

Suleiman did not say anything. He was frightened by the murderous expression in Mujahid's face. Though Mujahid had not said so, from the way he looked at him, he was sure Mujahid believed he was not a Moslem. His fears were soon confirmed.

'On the last day, God will begin his judgment with those who claim to be Moslems but are not,' he heard Mujahid saying. 'So-called Moslems are worse than non-Moslems and therefore more deserving of the sword on their throats. As God will start his judgment with this kind of Moslems, any jihad on earth should start with them. One should clean the house first before cleaning surroundings of the house.'

Again, Suleiman said nothing. If before he was afraid, now he was terrified. Mujahid holding a knife was looking like he would attack him with it. He had good reasons to fear. Mujahid had once told him how in a religious conflict between Moslems and Christians, he cut to pieces a Christian co-tenant. When he told him what he did, he was numb with shock

'Why would you do a thing like that?' he asked him when he could talk.

'The question should be why would I not do a thing like that,' Mujahid said. 'He was an infidel that deserved to die, and die painfully and brutally for his unbelief so that he tastes hell on earth before going to the hereafter for the real thing to be served on him.'

'But Christians are not infidels; the Quran calls them people of the book Moslems should not kill,' he said hoping to recover Mujahid from the fanatical hole he had fallen into.

'Yes, they are *ahl al-kitab* – people of the book; but they are also ahl-*dhimma* – infidels. As *dhimmis* – infidels, they are heirs to the sword,' Mujahid said in an impassioned voice. 'I don't think Allah in saying in the Quran that people of the book should not be killed really means what he says,' Mujahid said.

'Are you doubting Allah?' Suleiman asked shocked by what Mujahid said.

'I am not doubting him. I am only saying I don't think he means what he says in the Quran when he says we should not kill people of the book. I think he means something we are yet to understand.'

'This is unbelievable,' Suleiman muttered still looking shocked.

'If we don't kill people of the book, who will we kill?' he heard Mujahid saying.

'Must we kill?'

'I think we must. There is too much filth around the world for a true Moslem to breathe without choking. All one sees about him are swine.'

He initially thought what Mujahid said about killing Christians was his sole perversity, but when he considered how many Christians had been killed by Moslems during religious conflicts in the country and around the world, he wondered if all or at least most Moslems in the country and around the world were not thinking like Mujahid. Is Allah playing politics with

Christians by calling them people of the book Moslems should not kill? he wondered.

Now saying Moslems like him were worse than unbelievers, Mujahid could do worse things to him. With a Moslem like Mujahid, friendship like neighbourhood, did not count. What counted was the reward he would get in the hereafter if he could kill anyone he thought was not true to Islam. Moslems like him were volcanoes that could erupt without notice. He quickly walked away from the smouldering volcano.

Chapter Seven

Perhaps because of his experience with both, Mujahid hated the street and begging on it. Orphaned by a belief and educational system, Mujahid went early to the street and left it late. When the street talked, he was there; when it sang, he was there and when it wept, he was there. When strange spirits walked the street at night, he was also there. Though not born by the street, it was like he was born for it. Because he had an intimate relationship with the street, he knew it more than anyone.

To Mujahid, the street was a snake in more ways than one. In appearance, the street looked like a snake. In deviousness and wickedness, the street was a snake. Very few people on the street cared. Most people he approached on the street to beg for alms looked at him with contempt before walking or driving away without giving him anything. Some people before he even got close to them to beg, the contempt in their faces would put him off. Often their contempt irked him more than their refusal to give him anything. While not giving him anything, they would still look at him with contempt, why? It was like double punishment. It was ironical that it was people who gave him alms that did not look at him with contempt while those who did not give him looked at him with contempt. Because people had no mercy on him, he resolved to have no mercy for anyone.

One day, he and Dan'azumi were begging on the road moving between cars that had been brought to a halt by a traffic warden. When vehicles began to move, he narrowly missed being hit by a driver who seemed to have driven his car at him on purpose. But for his agility, the car would have crushed him. He cursed and swore vengeance.

'Why do the rich treat the poor so shabbily in this country?' he said to Dan'azumi while the two were walking on the pedestrian lane with their begging bowls in their hands.

'Because the poor are poor,' Dan'azumi said. 'Being poor recommends one for contempt.'

'Fine, we shall see,' Mujahid spat.

'What shall we see?' Dan'azumi asked alarmed by the passion of hate in Mujahid's voice and face.

'For now, just take *we shall see*,' Mujahid said in the same impassioned tone. 'When the time of seeing comes, you will see what *we shall see*.'

'Not all rich people are bad or mean to the poor,' Dan'azumi said trying to mollify his friend. 'Take Jazuli for example. 'Every fasting and Salah periods, he sells rice, millet and sorghum to the poor at half the prices these cereals are sold in the market.'

'Jazuli is a bad example of the generosity of the rich,' Mujahid said, tartly.

'Why?'

'Jazuli is a diabolical man. He gives things to the poor to keep them poor and make himself richer.'

'How?'

'When he gives a poor man anything, the luck and wealth that would have gone to the man would be appropriated by diabolism for him.'

'What! Where did you hear this one?'

'I move around and hear a lot.'

'Well, I don't believe what you are saying. It is all bad press, a whispering campaign by miserly rich people who cannot do what Jazuli is doing.

Unable to be as generous and benevolent like him, they take to this wicked smearing campaign.'

'Call it what you like; all I know is that the only good rich man is a dead one.'

'Again, you are not right there,' Dan'azumi said with a somewhat amused expression on his face. 'Some of the people you see in this north driving very expensive vehicles are not as rich as you think. In fact, some of them are beggars like us. Being beggars, they can't be passing alms they are given to us.'

'You are right there,' Mujahid said his dour face going a shade lighter. He had just called to mind what Sheikh Shuaibu said when the Governor of Noka called for a ban on begging. 'I have almost forgotten what Sheikh Shuaibu said about a year ago when the Governor of Noka called for a ban on begging.'

''What did he say? I can't remember,' Dan'azumi said.

'He asked which begging does the Governor want to ban: begging by small almajiris on the road or by big almajiris in limousines? After asking this question, he told the story of how a man driven in a jeep went from office to office in the federal capital begging for alms. As he was being driven on the road, he saw on the road crippled beggars propelling themselves on small carts with tyres begging him for money. He laughed to himself murmuring, 'this people do not know I am a beggar like them.'

Dan'azumi laughed. Mujahid chuckled. He rarely laughed no matter the humour.

'There is also the story of how some elders in the north paid the President of Jeddere a courtesy visit expecting he would give them money in the course of the visit and when he did not, one of them said he put his hand inside his big gown and was doing *uwaka* – fanning abuses at the President.'

Again, Dan'azumi laughed.

'Hearing how badly the first batch of elders fared, a second batch of elders also went to see the President carrying brown envelopes which they discreetly waved at him hoping he would get the message, but the President pretended not to understand.'

Dan'azumi laughed most heartily.

'We are all beggars in the north,' Mujahid said. 'We only differ in the status of our begging.

'*Maula*[*] is an entrenched culture here. During the last fasting period I was in the house of a rich man in this Azeri and was shocked to hear an able-bodied man saying that for the past two weeks he had not eaten in his house. All he did was to move from house to house to be fed. Fed, clothed and housed, most of our people don't feel the need to work. It is this begging culture that makes other tribes hold us in contempt, calling us *Aboki* – low people.'

'You are right,' Dan'azumi said.

'An Igbo man was quarrelling with his brother when the brother said the man would be reincarnated as a Hausa man in his next life. The man began crying saying, 'what have I done to you for you to wish me such an evil fate?'

Again, Dan'azumi laughed.

---

[*] sponging on other people

Chapter Eight

All his life, Mujahid had always wanted to belong to an Islamic movement that would rid the world of the filth in it – infidels and so-called Moslems. Even as a little boy in Gazali's madrasa, he had hoped to be part of such a movement, but the opportunity never came. Out of school, he kept hoping for the emergence of such a movement in Jeddere but it did not emerge. When it did not emerge, he began thinking of forming one himself. That was how he came to found Lakum-Hakum, a jihad movement that sought to rid Jeddere of infidels and so-called Moslems so that true Islam could be established.

Lakum-Hakum had its operational headquarters in Bungunu forest. To get members for his Jihad movement, Mujahid focused on recruiting young boys from madrasas and the streets – his native abodes. The boys he recruited were people without stakes in the peace and prosperity of Jeddere. *Slates to swords* and *streets to swords; bowls to blood and bowls to tears,* were the slogans of his recruitment.

His father a poor man had forty-eight children. There were many poor people like his father with children they couldn't cater for. These children end up homeless and hopeless in madrasas and the streets. On the street, these children were people with chips on their shoulders. He decided to recruit them for his Islamic campaign and let the chips fall where they may. These children were ticking time-bombs that could go off any moment. He recruited these time bombs to explode them with maximum casualty.

From Mujahid's understanding of human nature, there is nothing a human being needs like hope either for this world or the next. Hope is the rope people hang on to avoid falling into the pit of hopelessness, despair and depression. The rope of hope could also be turned into a rope that would hang people or strangle them. He would use hope in the hereafter as a rope to make children in madrasas and the streets hang onto life. He would also use the same rope to hang and strangle so-called Moslems and infidels in the *herenow*.

Hope is a lightning rod. All he needed do is to torch hope in the hereafter among hopeless children in madrasas and the streets of Jeddere would go up in flames. Slates in the hands of pupils of madrasas would turn to swords and bowls in their hands would be the receptacles blood from the striking swords would be collected.

'Madrasas and the streets have bred many urchins,' he said to Dan'azumi who he has convinced to be part of his insurgent group.

'That's very true,' Dan'azumi said. 'The street has bred many urchins.'

'These urchins are possessed by the wayward and harden demons of the street,' Mujahid mooed.

'But why does the street make people wayward and hardens them?' Dan'azumi asked. 'The street urchin is wayward and hardened; the prostitute also always on the street is wayward and hardened, why?'

'The street exposes both the urchin and prostitute to the mean, unsympathetic and devious nature of man,' Mujahid said. 'Meanness, lack of sympathy and deviousness are the water in the stream called the street. The urchin and prostitute have bathed in and drank this water all their lives. 'Meanness, lack of sympathy and deviousness are the poison that flow through the snake called the street. This poison has seeped into the veins of the urchin and the prostitute turning them into snakes that can strike anyone who steps on them or anyone they don't like.'

'There is a lot of truth in what you are saying,' Dan'azumi said.

'The same way vehicles moving on a road harden and break a road, the mean, unsympathetic and devious behaviour of people on the street harden and break the urchin and the prostitute on the street. Their hearts broken, neither the urchin nor the prostitute has any feelings for anyone. Because no one has shown he carries a heart that feels for them, they carry no heart that feels or cares for anyone. Broke in pocket and purse, they are broke in heart as well.'

For a while no one spoke. Dan'azumi was pondering what Mujahid just said. Mujahid on his part was recalling some of his mean action as a street urchin. Whenever he fetched water for anyone, he would urinate and spit in the water after looking round to ensure no one sees him doing any of these. Other madrasas pupils who did the same thing, he led them into doing so.

'They give us stale food, we will give them urine, spit and sputum as water,' he said to a madrasa pupil he had convinced into doing what he had been doing for a long time.

'What a dirty way to hit back!' the pupil exclaimed, laughing.

'The swine called the street has rubbed its back against us.'

'What a poisonous way to hit back!'

'The snake called the street has slithered into us with all its poison,' Mujahid said in a feverous tone. 'We will be smiting any water we sell to them with the poison in us.'

'They buy water from us thinking they are buying the showers of life ...'

'When they are in fact buying urine, spit and sputum. We will not eat alone the stale and poisonous food they give us. They will eat it with us.'

'My friend, you have really understood how the street impacts on the so-called street urchin and the prostitute,' Mujahid heard Dan'azumi saying while he was still recollecting his mean behaviour as a pupil of a madrasa and a street urchin.

'You can say that again and again, and not even *Kauku*[*] can fault you,' Mujahid said, returning from his journey into the past.

Chapter Nine

Years after they graduated from their madrasas, Mujahid and Suleiman met and began discussing Islam as was common with them.

'*Salaam* in Arabic means peace. It was from this word Islam was coined. So Islam means peace,' Suleiman said.

'I hear you,' Mujahid hissed.

'When you say *salamalaikum* on meeting anyone or entering a house, you are not only saying peace to the person or house, you are declaring Islam to the person or the house,' Suleiman said.

'You are right there,' Mujahid said. 'However, while it is good to declare Islam to an infidel or so-called Moslems with the hope of bringing them to the right path of Islam, it is a wrong thing saying peace to them,'

'Why is it wrong saying peace to them?' Suleiman asked a little surprised.

'Because an infidel and a so-called Moslem do not deserve peace,' Mujahid spat. 'All they deserve is war and that's why they are in the abode of war, not of peace.'

'So if you meet a so-called infidel and a so-called Moslem what do you say to him?' Suleiman, curious to know what Mujahid's answer will be, asked.

'Jihad,' Mujahid spat.

Though he had half-expected this answer, Suleiman was nonetheless shocked by it. '*A uzubilahi*!' he exclaimed.

For a while none of the two men said anything. They both seemed lost in their individual thoughts.

'Islam is a simple and easy religion to believe in and practice,' Suleiman said, breaking the silence.

'That's true,' Mujahid said.

'Why is Islam simple and easy to practice?' Suleiman asked.

Mujahid did not say anything.

'Islam is simple and easy to practice because it wants peace not only in the world, but even in the believer himself,' Suleiman continued. 'As a simple and easy religion, Islam is a religion of alternatives even in obligatory matters. Though you are required to pray standing, bending and squatting, if you are too sick to do any of these,

Islam allows you to pray sitting down on a chair. Though you are required to perform pilgrimage to Mecca, you don't have to discharge this obligation if you don't have the means. Though you are required to perform ablution with water, you can use sand to perform it if you can't find water. Though you are required to give alms, you are free of this obligation if you are without means of discharging it. I can go on and on. Islam is a religion of possibilities not impossibilities. It does not place on a believer a duty he cannot perform. Since it is not possible for everyone to be a Moslem, Islam the religion of possibilities will not insist on this.'

Still Mujahid did not say anything. Instead he sat mumbling to himself with a wild and fierce expression on his face. Inside his head the wasp was flying about with a buzzing sound.

'Islam is all peace,' Suleiman pursued.

'What you are saying was not what my teacher taught me,' Mujahid said with a ferocious look on his face.

'What did your teacher teach you?' Suleiman asked.

'He taught me that Islam is all war.'

'He taught you Islam is all war, what have you taught yourself, or you can't teach yourself?'

Mujahid did not say anything.

'Is it only what your teacher taught you, you will work with? Can't you think for yourself?' Suleiman probed further.

'To know Islam is war and not peace, check out how many peace pacts it has signed and how many wars it has fought,' Mujahid said as if he had not heard what Suleiman said.

'It has fought these wars not because it is war, but because of its warped understanding by people like you,' Suleiman said.

'No, no, no,' Mujahid screamed looking slate loose. 'Islam has fought these wars because it resents injustice.'

'Moslems are not the only ones who suffer injustice in the world,' Suleiman said in a very emotional voice. 'Shintos, Christians, Hindus, Buddhists and so many believers in other religions also suffer injustice. If you don't know, I will tell you that injustice is an integral part of life. Why are Moslems acting God? Why are they quick to pass judgment God will pass on the last day? Why are they foisting double jeopardy on so-called unbelievers?'

'Islam cannot tolerate any form of injustice,' Mujahid said, again as if he had not heard what Suleiman said.

'It means it can't tolerate life; life is full of injustice,' Suleiman said.

'Islam cannot live with injustice,' Mujahid repeated in an impassioned tone.

'Then it cannot live with life,' Suleiman said. 'If Islam cannot live with life, what will it live with?'

'Death,' Mujahid spat. 'True Islam lives with death; that's why it is always killing infidels and so-called Moslems.'

'I can't believe what I am hearing,' Suleiman said shocked by what Mujahid said.

'Islam cannot live with unbelief,' Mujahid said contempt flaring in his eyes like the flames of Ajuwo.* 'That's why it is in a permanent state of war with infidels and so-called Moslems.'

'In a permanent state of war, Islam is in a permanent state of death, and I will add in a

---

* The flames of Ajuwo were flames in Ajuwo mythology said to flare in long feverous waves.

permanent state of shame,' Suleiman said. 'We are not getting new coverts. The only Moslems we have are those born into the religion and we are killing them. If we continue the way we are, we will wake up one day and find there are no more Moslems and no more Islam the most beautiful religion in the world.'

Mujahid did not say anything. He relapsed into murmuring to himself while gritting his teeth.

'Death bred by your brand of Islam claims more Moslems than so-called infidels,' Suleiman went on after a while of silence. 'Take away death bred by your kind of Islam and Moslems would overrun the world. We marry four wives and give birth to more children. Take away death triggered by your brand of Islam and many people not born into the faith will flock to it. Islamic clergies do not extort money from their followers the way Christian clergies do; neither do they appear as wayward. Take away hate bred by your type of Islam and legions would troop to this thrilling religion. Your variety of Islam, while seeking to make everyone in the world a Moslem, is the reason people flee the faith. Can you see the tragic irony of your sort of Islam?'

Mujahid still did not say anything.

Suleiman also for a while did not say anything. His mind was recalling what Sufyan his teacher used to teach them about jihad. While Gazali was telling his pupils that jihad is part of faith and therefore part of the five pillars of Islam, Sufyan was also telling his own pupils the same thing. Also like Gazali, Sufyan told his pupils there were three forms of jihad: Jihad of the heart, of the mouth and of the hand. But while Gazali was telling his pupils that the best form of jihad is that of the hand, Sufyan was telling his own pupils the best form of jihad is that of the heart.

'Why is jihad of the heart the best form of jihad?' Suleiman asked.

'Because while engendering piety, this form of jihad does not endanger peace,' Sufyan said. 'Islam means peace. Whatever advances peace is Islam. Whatever endangers peace is not Islam. Peace can never be achieved through jihad of the hand and therefore this form of jihad is not Islam. If it is Islam, it is not obligatory Islam. It is not even recommendatory Islam; it is innovative Islam.'

A car drove past where the two friends were hooting loudly. The horn of the car snapped

Suleiman out of his thoughts into speaking out his thoughts, 'Islam is peace, not war,' he said. 'Because Islam is peace, jihad of the heart is the most noble and important jihad.'

'Islam is not only peace, it is also justice,' Mujahid countered. 'Peace as everyone knows is founded on justice.'

'Fine, Islam is justice and peace is anchored on justice; where is the injustice in anyone refusing to be a Moslem or even being an impious one that will move me to hate or kill him?' Suleiman asked. 'What injustice does a Moslem or Islam suffer if I refuse to be a Moslem or a good one?'

Mujahid did not say anything. It was not clear whether he was quiet because he could not answer Suleiman's question or for some other reason.

'This split vision in Islam, how long will it continue?' Suleiman wondered aloud. 'Islam is peace, Islam is war; salaam and jihad, where will it all end?'

Chapter Ten

Northern Jeddere which provided the human raw materials for Mujahid's Jihad was a region with abundant land and a teeming population of youths. Before settling for insurgency, Mujahid had several times wondered why state governments of the region were not taking advantage of the abundant land and population of the region. With so much youthful population and arable land, northern Jeddere should have done very well in agriculture. The government should have acquired massive acres of land and engage the youth either in the cultivation of cash crops or growing of economic trees. This sustained over time, would lead to an agricultural revolution that will require machines to process the crops and fruits harvested. Proceeds from sales of the crops and fruits produced and processed would be used to pay the wages of the youths working the land. There was land; there was a youthful population to till it. Why was there no marriage between the land and the youthful population? he wondered aloud one day to Dan'azumi

'Marriage between the land and the youthful population in northern Jeddere would have been a great idea,' Dan'azumi said impressed by Mujahid's wits that scared up this quaint analogy.

'Young men are quick to wed maidens but loathed to wed the land,' Mujahid pursued. 'Every weekend all you hear and see are wedding ceremonies between young men and maidens to produce children, but no wedding ceremonies between young men and the land to produce food.'

'The result is that many mouths are produced without food to feed them,' Dan'azumi said, rapidly.

'Harems and children everywhere; harvests and food nowhere,' Mujahid pursued with verve. 'Instead of slating and bowling, youths in northern Jeddere should be hoeing and weeding.'

'You are saying a lot of fresh things today,' Dan'azumi said looking at Mujahid admirably. Though he had always known Mujahid as a witty person, today he seemed electric in thought as witty.

In the countryside of northern Jeddere, wherever one looked, all one saw was land stretching to the end of his vision. An Igbo man in northern Jeddere on hearing people were litigating over land wondered why they should when land was everywhere.

Most of the land in northern Jeddere was uncultivated though there were plenty hands to cultivate it. The region was bursting with a teeming population of young people who for the most part were idle hands. Whenever any untoward thing happened in Azeri, young people poured into the scene the thing was happening as if they were vomited by the earth. Every Friday, young people poured into the street for Friday prayers. During Sallah festival, mammoth crowds of young people lined the street to watch the emir and other traditional title holders ride on horses' backs in a durbar procession. During one of these durbar processions, Mujahid and Dan'azumi were among the young people who lined the road the emir, traditional title holders and their children would ride through. For a long time, they waited in the hot scorching sun by the roadside for the durbar procession to show up but it did not until evening. When it showed up, Mujahid was tired and irritable. Waziri and his followers who usually led such processions were the first to appear. Mujahid viewed them in a hazy, blurred gaze that reduced them to distant flickering, pale images shorn of the pomp and pageantry they plied. Most horses were ridden on; but a few horses had no riders.

Horses with riders had people walking beside them holding leading strings tied to the horses. Those riding the horses were royals, while those trekking beside the horses holding leading strings were commoners.

The few horses without riders also had people holding their leading strings leading them along the road. A thought that had never engaged Mujahid now engaged him. On the heels of this thought was a festering and seething resentment. 'Why would some human beings be riding horses while others are trekking even when there were horses without riders?' he said, involuntarily.

'Because this is how the world is made,' Dan'azumi said. 'In this you can see the rude and naked working of the saying that if wishes were horses, beggars will ride.'

'Who made the world like this?'

'I suppose God.'

'No, God did not make the world this way. This is all the cruel handiwork of man.'

For a while none of the two friends spoke. It seemed they were both caught up in their individual thoughts.

Standing near the two friends and listening to their conversation was a young man who looked like he had good western education. Though he had been listening to the conversation with rising interest, he had not said anything yet. By the various shades of expression that flowed in and out of his face, he looked like he held the procession before him in contempt. When the two young men he had been listening to their conversation fell into silence, he broke the silence. 'All humans are humus,' he said in an arid haunting tone. 'When alive, being is added to humus and so you have human being. When dead, being goes leaving only humus,' he continued talking in the same arid, haunting tone.

'That's very true,' Mujahid said. 'Why then should one humus ride while another is trekking?

'Because one humus has blue blood while the other has only red blood,' the young man said. 'Those hewing wood with their hands are those now hewing the road with their feet. Those drawing and trucking water with their hands are those trucking the horses with their hands and the road with their feet.'

'And they seem happy doing so,' Dan'azumi said.

'In their ignorance and stupidity, they are happy no doubt,' the young man said.

'Feudalism can only breed feuds,' Mujahid said. The feudalist set up in the north can only breed resentment, bitterness and anger in the oppressed poor.'

'The entire set up is unacceptable,' Dan'azumi said.

'We will not remain the hewers of wood and drawers of water for much longer,' Mujahid said. 'Very soon, we will no longer hew wood, we will hew people; we will no longer draw water, we will draw blood.'

'What you are saying reminds me of a story of the Emir of Noka that I heard a few days ago,' Dan'azumi said.

'Please tell me the story, I am all ears,' Mujahid said in an eager voice.

'Some young men were brought to the emir of Noka for punishment because they insulted the emir. When the emir was told the offence of the young men, he asked his guards to let them go. The guards were shocked by the emir's action as they released the youngsters. After the youngsters had departed, the emir summoned his cabinet to a meeting where he talked on the respect bordering on reverence that used to exist between the *talakawas** and royalty in the past. According to the emir, *talakawas* used to wait by the wayside in the hope they will see the emir if they had information the emir would be passing that way on a certain day. If they had the fortune of seeing the emir, they would go home happy they had seen the emir in their life time. If today children whose parents or grandparents used to wait for the emir by the wayside were insulting the emir, it meant something was wrong. It meant there was something the emir or his emirate was not doing right that had bred this contempt.

'What a tale!' Mujahid exclaimed, looking excited.

'It was the same thing I said when I heard the tale,' Dan'azumi said.

Instead of cultivating its vast arable lands as Mujahid had envisaged, northern Jeddere allowed

---

* Poor, common people that are not from royal families

the land lie fallow. Instead of engaging its youthful population in the land, the population was left idle. Finding land fallow and population idle, Mujahid decided to find engagement for both. Fallow land that had turned into forest would be used to camp idle hands he was recruiting into insurgency. It was not only the idle mind that was the devil's workshop, idle land was also his workshop. He was the devil that will use these workshops. A hungry man is not only an angry man, he is an unreasonable man. He would exploit this anger and unreasonableness.

Chapter Eleven

Bungunu forest where Mujahid's Lakum-Hakum headquarters was, was in the northwest of Jeddere. The forest was a long and wide stretch of jungle one could easily get lost in. Composed of groves, caves and tunnels, the forest was a treacherous wilderness with hiding places and bobby traps. It was this quality of the forest that made Mujahid chose it as the place to have his operational headquarters. While he and his men could easily find their targets in town, they could not easily be found by the military with who they were in guerrilla warfare. Located to advantage, government troops looking for them could easily get lost or fall into a bobby trap in the forest making them easy targets for him and his men.

'This jungle is so cool and comforting,' Mujahid said to Dan'azumi when they first went on a survey of the forest.

'It is,' Dan'azumi said. 'It affords good cover against aerial attacks.'

'It sure does,' Mujahid said. 'In a jungle like this, you can move camp even in the day without much fear of detection. You can hide in a cave or tunnel taking pot-shots at the enemy without much care of being hit. The whole forest gives me the feeling of being in a bunker of trees.'

'My surprise is how a jungle like this has been able to prosper so well in the Savanah,' Dan'azumi said.

'Once you don't fell trees, even the shrub in the course of time will become a tree,' Mujahid said.

'That's true,' Dan'azumi said.

'There are many obstacles between one and bullets here,' Mujahid said. 'There are also many bunkers to retreat into. In this forest, I have a feeling of being a tortoise that can easily recoil into its shell when attacked.'

'We can easily go to them; they can't easily come to us,' Dan'azumi said. 'We can see them; they can't see us. Even the sun cannot easily see us here. In all these lies the beauty of this jungle and the good it holds for us, if it holds calamity for others.'

'It is so fitting to purpose,' Mujahid said.

'If you get lost in this jungle, the demons in it will not have mercy on you,' Dan'azumi said, laughing.

'It is as if it was created with our mission in mind,' Mujahid said. 'It is so much to purpose.'

'What you just said reminds me of what someone said when a certain young man was called hopeless,' Dan'azumi said.

'What did he say?' Mujahid asked with rare excitement.

'He said though the young man was not in existence when the word hopeless was coined, whoever coined the word had the young man in mind when he coined it,' Dan'azumi said.

Mujahid chuckled. He walked away from Dan'azumi to a nearby tree and to Dan'azumi's surprise swarmed up the tree with the agility of a monkey. When he got to where the tree forked out into branches, he sat on the fork and surveyed the forest around him, gleefully. 'This forest is simply great!' he wailed.

'You are also great climbing the tree the way you did,' Dan'azumi said, looking at Mujahid with admiration. 'A monkey cannot do what you did faster. I was with you on the ground, then I saw you on a tree.'

"Swarming up trees is one of my special skills just as shooting without missing is,' Mujahid said beaming at Dan'azumi. 'If we must survive in this forest, we must learn how to swarm up trees like monkeys and scurry into holes like bandicoot rats. The forest is a sea of trees; to prosper in it one must be able to swim well among the trees. The happy thing is that the skill is not so difficult to acquire.'

'I will learn from you.'

'And I will teach you.'

The opportunity Mujahid had been looking for to form an Islamic insurgent group came from two unexpected quarters. The first was a mercenary war in Dukwa. When the struggle to topple Maidu'a the President of Dukwa began, Mujahid did not pay much attention to it. It was when the struggle was about toppling Maidu'a that he saw an opportunity in the tussle and got interested. Maidu'a was looking for mercenaries to stem the rising tide of the rebels that were fighting for his ouster. Mujahid crossed the border between Jeddere and Dukwa to offer himself as a mercenary, not because he liked Maidu'a but because he liked the gun and money he would get from him. Far from liking Maidu'a, he despised him and wanted him toppled. So when he collected money and a gun from Maidu'a, he switched loyalty to the rebels and fought like the dickens during the war. When Maidu'a was toppled and the war was over, he returned to Jeddere with his gun and some money only to be recruited as a thug in Bangara's electioneering campaign.

To win his re-election, Governor Bangara who had become very unpopular because of poor performance in his first term as Governor, resorted to recruiting thugs to help him win through electoral malpractices. He armed the thugs with guns for them to invade polling units and collation centers to snatch ballot boxes and result sheets. After the election which he won, he sought to disband the thugs, but found he could not.

Mujahid who had thought he would have to stretch himself to recruit madrasa pupils he would have to acquire weapons for and train, suddenly found himself with a core military unit of armed thugs he did not have to train or arm. These thugs formed the nucleus of his insurgency. Madrasas pupils he later recruited, he recruited as an expansion of his military campaign against the Jeddere state.

Chapter Twelve

Though he had guns and people he could recruit to wage jihad against infidels and so-called Moslems, Mujahid knew he also needed a lot of money. Jihad is a suicide mission. Though there were those who embark on it simply because they hate infidels and so-called Moslems or because they believe they are answering the call of Allah to advance Islam, a good number of jihadists only participate in Jihad if they are paid. It was from Gazali his teacher he first learned of this category of jihadists. All the while he had always thought Jihad was a volunteer activity by sincere Moslems committed to advancing Islam with making paradise as their only remuneration. He was therefore shocked to learn that some jihadists insist on earthly remuneration as well.

'But why would anyone ask to be paid before he would participate in a jihad?' he asked in bewilderment.

'Because he believes Jihad is not his cause; but Allah's cause,' Gazali said. 'Because mercenary jihadists believe jihad is not their cause, they not only insist on being paid, but being paid well. If they would die fighting for this cause, they should be well paid for doing so, so that their widows and children would live on what they were paid.

'Who do they want to pay them?' he asked in bewilderment.

'Whoever is inviting them to undertake the jihad,' Gazali said.

'But it is Allah who asks them to do jihad,' he said still looking confounded.

'That's true,' Gazali said. 'But someone on earth is telling them to answer Allah's call. It is the person telling them to answer the call that should pay.'

'I would have thought the person reminding one of his duty should be thanked and not required to pay for reminding one of his duty,' Mujahid remonstrated.

'That's how it should be, but unfortunately is not,' Gazali said.

'It is sad,' Mujahid said in a bitter tone. 'I think some jihadists require jihad to be waged against them also.'

'You are right,' Gazali said. 'Jihadists always need purification. Jihads always need jihad also.'

Unfortunate and annoying as he found the demand of some jihadists to be paid money before embarking on jihad, Mujahid eventually had to accept this irksome reality. Having accepted the bitter reality, he began wondering where he would get money to fund the jihad movement he wanted to establish. It was while he was still scratching his head on how he would come by funds to undertake a jihad that he stumbled on Bital Adili a terrorist organization in Diran with a vision of global jihad. This organization had promotion of jihad activities around the world as its sole and fundamental mission.

It was from Sidjani, a fellow mercenary in the Dukwa rebellion that Mujahid got to know about Bital Adili. During the rebellion, he fought alongside Sidjani. In the course of the fighting they became friends. After the rebellion they both went back to their countries but maintained contact. It was in the course of maintaining contact that Sidjani introduced him to the organization when he intimated him of his intention to wage a jihad in Jeddere.

'Bital Adili will be happy to fund you,' Sidjani had said.

'Who is Bital Adili?' he had asked.

'Bital Adili is a terrorist organization in Diran with a vision of global jihad,' Sidjani had said.

'Are you serious about what you are saying?'

'I am damn serious,' Sidjani said in a firm tone.

'How can I access this organization?' Mujahid asked, his heart beating fast with excitement. What he was hearing was too good to be true.

'I can introduce you to Bital Adili,' Sidjani said.

'Just like that?' Mujahid said; he was beginning to wonder if he was sleeping and dreaming or awake. He had not known Sidjani for a long time; why should he extend such a favour to him? Was there even an organization like the one Sidjani was talking about? The whole thing was sounding like a fairy tale.

'Just like that,' Sidjani said.

'To Bital Adili then,' Mujahid said.

After verifying his claim of being a jihadist, Mujahid was amazed how willing Bital Adili was to fund his jihad. The organization was ready to give money and logistics of effecting his purpose. As soon as he assembled resources for the jihad, Mujahid swung into action.

True to his words, so-called Moslems were the first to be hit by Mujahid's jihad. His first attack was on a mosque during Friday congregational prayers. The central mosque in Lakuta was a very popular mosque. It attracted more worshippers than any mosque in northern Jeddere particularly on Fridays. Lakuta a very populous city was a Moslem city. In addition, it was a junction city through which many travellers passed. On a Friday, Moslem travellers stopping over to pray in Lakuta mosque banding together with the people of the city turned the mosque into a beehive bustling with people.

The bomb Mujahid used to attack Lakuta central mosque was built by Baqil. Baqil was a Lebanese who built most of the bombs used in the Syrian war. No bomb built by him ever failed to achieve maximum devastation of lives and property when detonated.

The Friday Lakum-Hakum bombed the central mosque in Lakuta was a very hot day. It was one of those days in northern Jeddere the sun bled heat on earth making people wonder if hell was leaking over their heads. If they wondered so this Friday, they did not have to wonder long. Mujahid's Lakum-Hakum soon led hell loose in Lakuta Central mosque.

Chapter Thirteen

The ten thousand pounds bomb was shipped in a hearse-like vehicle people thought was carrying rubbish for disposal. People in Lakuta were used to these kinds of vehicles moving through the city carrying rubbish. So no one paid it much attention as it inched closer to the mosque. Close to the mosque surrounded by people, the vehicle stopped. Its driver came out as if to find out why the vehicle stopped and the bomb went off. The bang generated by the bomb was so loud it seemed not only the ground shook, but the sky as well. People hit more violently by the bomb were tossed into the air falling back to the ground in bits and pieces. Pieces of human flesh and broken bones were strewn near and far where the bomb detonated while blood flowed on the road like water through arteries in a delta.

Those hit by the bomb but not killed, either limped about in shock and confusion crying or lay on the ground groaning in pain. Those not killed or injured were running away from the scene of the blast screaming and shrieking. The bomb has ignited the mosque. Flames of fire and smoke were billowing out of it in flaring waves and dense rolls of fog that were suffocating and asphyxiating. In the sky, smoke emitted by the blast and the fire it ignited spiralled and fanned out into the neighbourhood like refugees from hell. Within a short time the vicinity of the mosque that was a while ago a melee of people was a forlorn and deserted place.

About half a kilometre away from the bombed mosque, two people who were in the mosque but escaped the bombing unscathed, stood looking at the burning mosque in shock and disbelief. None of them could explain how they escaped without a scratch. All they could remember was that they heard a deafening bang and began running without knowing where they were running to.

Looking about them, they could see maimed people that had managed to drag themselves away from the scene of the carnage. A man who had lost one of his legs to the bomb was dragging himself backward on his buttocks, waving his hand about and screaming, 'no, no, no,' as if the bomb that maimed him was still coming after him and he was waving it away in terror. Moving backward on his buttocks, it was clear he couldn't have brought himself where he was. Someone must have brought him.

Further down where the man with the amputated leg was, a man who lost part of his face to the bomb was looking sightlessly about him. He was groaning in such a heart-wrenching manner that would not fail to break the heart of anyone seeing him and hearing his agony.

A little boy struck in the arm by shrapnel from the bomb was running around in pain holding his injured arm. His white clothes had turned crimson with blood. It was difficult understanding why he was running around instead of standing or sitting in one place or even walking away.

'Why God, why?' one of the two men that escaped the blast unscathed mourned, his body soaked in sweat.

'Who could have done this?' the other man wailed heaving and panting. Like the man with him, he too was soaked in sweat.

'Who else, but our fellow Moslems,' the first man said. 'It is only our people that throw bombs in this country. I just can't understand why they keep embarrassing and scandalizing our peaceful and noble religion like this.'

'Neither can I,' the second man said. 'How do you hope to attract people to your religion by violence? 'Do people embrace people wearing bombs or they run away from them? It is difficult understanding how these guys think.'

'I don't think they are after attracting people to the faith,' said the first man. 'If they were, they won't be attacking Moslems.'

'That's where you are wrong,' said the second man. 'They don't see you as a Moslem.'

'Neither do I see them as Moslems,' the first man, spat.

'For them, you are just another infidel they want to terrorise into accepting Islam,' said the second man.

'It is so disgraceful,' said the first man. 'Even I born into the faith keep wondering whether I should leave when the shame of this kind of action gets to me. How then will anyone not born into the religion accept it?'

'You suffer the disgrace you are talking about alone,' said the second man. 'Suffering the disgrace alone, these guys see you as a disgrace.'

'How can Islam flourish with this type of behaviour by people who call themselves Moslems?' the first man lamented. 'Buddhism, Shintoism and Christianity are peaceful, why is the situation different with our own faith?'

'If they are bride-maids putting earrings on Islam, time will tell,' said a man standing behind the two men. 'If they are beautifying Islam, Islam will be the beautiful damsel it should be. If on the contrary they are mad dogs that are biting off the ears of Islam and running away with them, time will also tell. Islam will live with the scar for the rest of its life.'

'You have said something there,' said the second man.

The third man did not say anything. It seemed he did not even hear what the second man said, for he was walking away towards the man with the amputated leg to see if he could help him.

Chapter Fourteen

After the mosque bombing, there were wildcat bombings of churches, police and military establishments by Lakum-Hakum. The attacks caught both the police and military napping. In the confusion they woke up, they spun round in panic and hysteria. Police stations and army institutions were barricaded with sand-filled drums and iron bars. Police that were supposed to put others behind bars, found themselves behind bars.

The day Lakum-Hakum stormed a police station in Tawaki for a long time remained a memorable one with the public if an embarrassing one with the police. The insurgents armed with AK47, grenades and other sophisticated weapons for close to an hour bombarded the station with heavy artillery fire in waves after waves of attack.

Initially, the police responded with gunshots from the station. But after eight or nine policemen were shot dead by the insurgents, no shot was again heard coming from the police station. All that was heard were a barrage of gunfire from the insurgents who kept moving closer to the station. A hand propelled grenade ripped off the front roof of the station. Another grenade tore through the ceiling of the station where the roof had been torn off. The second grenade landed on a policeman hiding in the station and blew off his head. Five or six policemen in fright and panic ran out of the station screaming and shrieking in wild terror. They were all tossed into the air by a torrent of bullets from the firing guns of the insurgents.

Soon the insurgents were inside the station. Inside the station, they were no longer shooting; instead they were flushing out policemen hiding in toilets and cupboards and bringing them outside the station where they shot them. The last batch of police they found in the station, they lined up and ordered them to file out of the station with their hands on their heads. Outside the station, they ordered them to frog-jump before shooting all of them except four. The four that were not shot included the Divisional Police Officer and the Crime Division Officer. The four police officers were ordered by the insurgents to crawl about the station's courtyard and bark like dogs. They did as they were ordered. As they crawled about, Sa'adu the insurgent who led the attack on the station commanded them to repeat after him whatever he said.

'We are dogs of infidels,' Sa'adu said.

'We are dogs of infidels,' the police officers crawling about repeated what the insurgent leader had said.

'We are dogs of pigs.'

'We are dogs of pigs.'

'We have lost our teeth to corruption and cannot bite.'

'We have lost our teeth to corruption and cannot bite.'

'We cannot even bark well.'

'We cannot even bark well.'

'We are useless.'

'We are useless.'

'All governments of Jeddere are infidel governments.'

'All governments of Jeddere are infidel governments.'

'We the dogs of these infidel governments deserve to rot in hell.'

'We the dogs of these infidel governments deserve to rot in hell.'

After they finished insulting themselves and the government, they were asked to beg for their lives. Kicked about by the insurgents they begged to be spared death. They were not spared. They were all shot dead. After shooting them, they set what remained of the station ablaze before speeding away in their vehicles.

When the insurgents left the police station, the whole place was littered with corpses of policemen and women in their uniforms. It was a sordid and frightful sight.

For days, the print and electronic media were agog with news of the invasion of Tawaki police station by the insurgents. The manner of the attack and what the insurgents did to the police at the station had never been heard in the country and indeed anywhere in the world.

For days, the federal government did not say anything about the attack. People said the government was numb with shock and shame as people were. What the insurgents did to the police station and the police therein not only showed how audacious and ruthless they were, it showed the deep contempt they had for authority. It also showed how weak and cowardly the police were.

'The police has once more shown they cannot even protect themselves, lest anyone,' a man said to his neighbour.

'What happened at Tawaki police station was indeed shameful and disgusting,' the neighbour said. 'This disgraceful level of incompetence is what corruption has done to Jeddere police.'

'Caught with their pants down, the police could not draw their pants up to cover their nudity,' said the first man. 'Standing disgustingly with their pants down, they were feeding everyone with the shame of their nudity.'

'It is sad.'

It is indeed sad.'

Chapter Fifteen

The horror and scandal of Lakum-Hakum insurgents attack on the police station had scarcely died down when the insurgents invaded a female secondary school in the small town of Yagurza and abducted some of the students. The school was one of the few surviving missionary schools in Jeddere. Located at the outskirts of the small town across a stream, the school was one of the old and famous female schools in Jeddere.

In all, over three hundred students were abducted by the insurgents. Most of the students abducted were teenagers between the ages of fourteen and eighteen.

The abduction of the girls sparked global outrage. The abduction not only shocked Jeddere, it shocked the world. Though the invasion of the police station and the humiliation of the police was as unprecedented as the abduction of the girls, for a number of reasons, the sacking of the police station and the humiliation of the police did not spark the indignation and horror the abduction of the girls did.

First, the police were trained and armed adults that should not only be able to defend themselves, they should be able to defend others. If they could do neither, too bad. The abducted girls on the other hand were innocent, unarmed school children easy to pick. Secondly, as security agents that propped up the state which the insurgents were fighting, the police were natural targets for the insurgents. Not so the girls. The girls were totally outside the politics of the state. Thirdly, the girls were Christian girls and the insurgents were Moslems. The abduction of the girls by the insurgents was a declaration of war by Islam on Christianity. The fact that the school was a mission school further deepened the religious undertones of the abduction.

While the general public in and outside Jeddere deplored the abduction of the girls, Christians in and outside Jeddere raised Cain and hell over it. Christianity has once more been insulted and desecrated by the uncircumcised sons of Ishmael. There were calls for crusade to tackle the jihad Christians were groaning under. The Papacy in Rome threatened to shut down all its schools in Jeddere.

A pastor and an elder of his church met after the abduction of the girls and began talking about the kidnap.

'This time, the Ishmaelites have gone for the elephant's head,' the pastor said.

'What they did is what should not be told in Gath lest the daughters of the Philistines, lest the sons of the uncircumcised rejoice,' the elder said. 'Counsel for this kind of thing can only come from one hell of a being: the devil.'

'Imagine the agony of the parents of these girls. Just put yourself in their position. What can be more traumatising to a parent than his child being abducted by these fiends, a female child for that matter?' the pastor agonized.

'You can bet your farm on it that they will use their uncircumcised and unsterilized sticks to pollute these girls,' the elder said.

'It was said one of them in public glare copulated with the statue of Virgin Mary at the school while poking his sword at baby Jesus,' the pastor said his face contorting into an ugly tablet of hate and revulsion. 'This tells you what they will do to the girls.'

'You don't mean it pastor,' the elder said shock and disbelief branded on his face like terror tattoos.

'Unless the person who told me the story lied and I can't see why he should lie to me, that was what happened,' the pastor said.

'If they did what you just told me, they did what the devil will not do and I can tell you they will suffer nemesis the devil never suffered.'

All over Jeddere and outside it, there was grave indignation and outpour of curses, not only on the insurgents but on Islam and Moslems generally. It took the intervention of Amnesty International to douse in Christendom the flames puffed by the abduction of the girls.

In the insurgents' camps, the day the girls were abducted was a day of carousing, fanfare and debauchery – serial rapes of the girls.

'Since the daughters of infidels no longer want to marry us, we will abduct and rape them,' Mujahid said after raping three of the girls.

'That way we will be planting the seeds of Islam inside them,' an insurgent said, laughing.

'From now on, we shall be abducting and raping their girls so that they give birth to

Moslems. There is Islam in the milk we pour inside them. Since people are not converting to Islam, this is the only way to make up our declining numbers.'

'Children born from what we are now doing will look for their fathers,' another insurgent said. 'When they do so, they will find us and we will make Moslems of them if they are not already so.'

Dan'azumi was conspicuously missing in the raping of the girls. He had advised against the abduction of the girls, but no one heeded him. 'According to Mujahid, in jihad every weapon and every action is legitimate, particularly when you are fighting with your back to the wall as we are,' he said, beaming with rare satisfaction.

'But the Quran clearly says in war, we should spare children and women,' Dan'azumi said.

'The Quran says so when you are not fighting with your back to the wall,' Mujahid said.

'You keep saying we are fighting with our backs to the wall, which wall are we fighting with our backs to?' Dan'azumi asked, anger making his voice to tremble.

'If you can't see it, I can see and even touch it,' Mujahid said waving his hand about as if feeling the wall he said he could see and touch.

Chapter Sixteen

In Katiru village where Mujahid came from, his parents had become outcasts of sort because of their son's insurgency. Not many people wanted to have anything to do with them. Some people went as far as not wanting to pray in the same mosque with Naziru his father. One day his father was in his local mosque to pray when he suddenly found himself alone in the mosque. Other people including the imam had fled the mosque. This had never happened to him or indeed to anyone before. The worse people had done to him before now was to avoid praying beside him in the mosque but not flee the whole mosque. He was shocked, saddened and angered at the same time. Angered not only against his son but everyone, he swore at everyone. What was his crime in the matter? Was he the insurgent or did he ask his son to carry out the campaign of insurgency? Was he any less a victim of his son's insurgency than anyone?

After the mosque incident, Mujahid's mother went to the market to buy meat but found no butcher willing to sell meat to her. A butcher even mocked her that with so much meat of human beings, he was surprised she still wanted to buy meat of cows. She went back home crying.

Given the kind of hostility his family was under in Katiru, Naziru feared for himself and his family. People might go beyond hating them to killing them. But where would he run to with a large family like his? The mud house he had in Katiru was the only one he had in the whole world. Where then was he to take his mammoth family? He felt pursued and cornered. He went to his friend Jamilu to discuss his problem. Even if the whole world rejected and fled him, Jamilu would not do so. He was right. Jamilu received him in his house, though not as warmly as he used to.

'My family and I are gradually becoming ostracized in Katiru,' he lamented to Jamilu in a melancholic tone.

'I am afraid this is what I am seeing,' Jamilu said, a little coldly.

'We are becoming taboos and outcasts in our own land,' he mourned in a very abject tone.

'I am afraid this is what I am seeing,' Jamilu said.

'We have been tattooed with my son's abominable actions,' he whined, his head slumped on his chest.

'I am afraid this is what it seemed,' Jamilu said. 'The worse thing is that the tattooing is going beyond you to anyone who deals with you.'

Naziru's heart skipped a beat. Though he knew what Jamilu said to be the case or at least suspected it to be the case, hearing it from Jamilu shocked and frightened him. When ostracism goes beyond a person to those who deal with him, the person cannot live in the society ostracizing him because gradually everyone for his own good will forsake him. Given what Jamilu had just said, he could not count on him accepting him into his house for long. Already he could notice a marked coldness in Jamilu's attitude towards him. 'What is my own crime in this?' he wailed.

'Having too many children; that's your crime,' Jamilu said. 'You have children you can't take care of; this is the result.'

'I am beginning to wonder if that boy is my son,'Naziru said, sweat breaking out on his forehead.

'As for being your son, I have no doubt Mujahid is your son,' Jamilu said.

'If he is indeed my son, why is he doing what I can never contemplate?' Naziru said. 'No, that boy is not my son. His mother must have pulled a fast one on me.'

'Like I said before, Mujahid is your son,' Jamilu said. 'Don't smear the honour of a nobble woman. 'You sired Mujahid; but after siring him, you handed him to the street to also sire him. So he is not only your son; he is also the son of the street. You gave him biology; the street gave him sociology. The wayward behaviour he is exhibiting was bred in him by the street if not by you. You shouldn't be surprised if another of your children sired by the street follows Mujahid's path tomorrow.'

'But I am not the only one with many children on the street,' Naziru remonstrated.

'True, you are not the only one with children on the street,' Jamilu said. 'In fact, your case is the norm, not the exception in northern Jeddere. Most of those your son recruits into Lakum-Hakum are street urchins like him. I will not be surprised if they are his street mates.'

"I am not the only person with children on the street; why is my case this bad?' Naziru moaned, again.

'You are right to wonder why your case should be this bad; but you are also wrong. Everyone has his luck as everyone has his name. Two people eat the same food, one vomits; the other belches to express satiety.'

'God, forgive me my mistakes and have mercy on me and my family,' Naziru prayed with his eyes fixed to the ground.

'Amen,' Jamilu said.

'Mujahid if you have ever been my son, you are no longer my son,' Naziru swore.

'No, that's not the way to go,' Jamilu said. 'He is still your son. Rather pray that God should make a better son out of him.'

'Since this calamity has befallen me and my family because they said you are my son, you are no longer my son,' Naziru continued as if he had not heard what Jamilu said.

'I repeat, this is not the right way to go,' Jamilu said.

'I am the one wearing the shoes and therefore the one who knows the blisters they are giving my feet,' Naziru griped. 'Mujahid, you are cursed from this day. No good thing will ever come out of your life if indeed you are my son.'

Jamilu sighed in distress.

Chapter Seventeen

While Mujahid was prosecuting jihad of the hand in the name of Islam as he understood it, Suleiman was prosecuting jihad of the heart in the name of Islam as he understood it. Suleiman was not an imam of a particular mosque. Instead, he was an itinerant preacher who moved from town to town preaching the Islam of peace.

'From name to substance Islam is peace,' he said in a town he had gone to preach. 'This peace is attainable only through jihad of the heart. If for instance we all hate adultery, murder, lying, betrayal, theft and corruption, there would be peace on earth. This is what jihad of the heart requires all Moslems to do.

'When you sleep with somebody's wife or even desire her, you are not making the victim of your action love you; you are making him hate you. If you commit adultery and people know you are a Moslem, their hatred for you may extend to your religion. Hate is not peace; hate is war. Instead of making Islam the religion of peace it is, you are making it a religion of war it is not. But if by jihad of the heart, you resent adultery, you are making Islam a peaceful and attractive religion. By this action, you are waging jihad for Islam not against it.

'When you kill another person's relation in a religious conflict for example, you don't by doing so make the person whose relation you killed love you or Islam in whose name you killed the person; you make him hate you and Islam your religion. In fact, you make him hate the religion than you since he may not even know you. You have by your action made a beautiful and attractive religion ugly and repulsive. You have by your action waged jihad against Islam, not for it. But if by jihad of the heart, you resent killing people, you are making Islam a peaceful and attractive religion. By this action, you are waging jihad for Islam not against it.

'When you lie to anyone, you make him hate you, not love you. If he knows you are a Moslem, his hatred may go beyond you to your religion. In such a situation, instead of waging jihad for Islam, you are waging jihad against Islam. But if by jihad of the heart, you resent lies and tell the truth and people know you are a Moslem, you are making the religion beautiful and attractive. In such a situation you are waging jihad for the religion, not against it.

'When you betray anyone, the person you betrayed will not love you; he will hate you. If he knows you are a Moslem, his hatred may extend beyond you to your religion. If this happens, you are not waging jihad for Islam but against it. But if by jihad of the heart you resent betrayal, you are waging jihad for Islam, not against it.

'When you steal anyone's property or money, the victim will not like you; he will hate you. If he knows you are a Moslem, his hatred may go beyond you to your religion. Hatred is not peace; hatred is war. By theft, you will be waging war against Islam instead of for it. But if by jihad of the heart, you resent stealing, you will be fighting jihad for Islam, not against it.

'When you are corrupt, you don't make victims of your corruption love you; you make them hate you. If they know you are a Moslem, their hatred may go beyond you to your religion. If this happens, you are waging jihad against Islam, not for it. But if by jihad of the heart you resent corruption, you are fighting jihad for Islam, not against it.

'With peace on earth generated by jihad of the heart, everyone is already in heaven because heaven is all about peace. It is this peace generated by jihad of the heart that makes Islam a religion of peace and one that takes one to heaven.

'There is no hypocrisy in jihad of the heart. That's why it is the most difficult jihad to prosecute. Any hypocrite can prosecute jihad of the mouth and hand. Many people I know today who are prosecuting jihad of the mouth and hand don't even prosecute jihad of the heart. This people are fighting Islam, not fighting for it.

'Islam does not pick quarrels with anyone; people pick quarrels with Islam. Islam does not pick fights with anyone; people pick fights with Islam. Islam is one with nature and nature is peace.'

From city to city, Suleiman carried his brand of Islam. Perhaps because of the quick result he wanted to see but was not seeing, it seemed to Suleiman that he was not making the much-needed impact of swaying many people to his version of Islam the way Mujahid was swaying them to his.

'We for peace in Islam seemed to be winning the argument in sense, while those rooting for war are winning it in folly,' he said to himself in frustration one day after delivering one of his most powerful sermons without seeing the result he wanted to see. 'I hate using this expression, but I am compelled to use it: perhaps I should have left pigs to their wallowing.'

Though dismayed that his version of Islam wasn't enjoying the traction he saw that of Mujahid was, Suleiman never gave up on his own version. He went on preaching his version throughout the length and breadth of Jeddere.

Chapter Eighteen

While it was not difficult knowing why Suleiman took to the field against Mujahid, it was difficult understanding why Gazali – Mujahid's teacher, also started preaching against his pupil. Mujahid's brand of radical Islam was no doubt inspired by Gazali. Having its inspirational roots in Gazali's madrasa, at the beginning of Mujahid's insurgency, Gazali on two occasions visited his former pupil in his operational headquarters to further inspire and urge him on. However, as the insurgency grew fiercer, Gazali started showing less support for it until it was clear he was no longer in support of the insurgency. Why then did Gazali began preaching against Mujahid's insurgency?

It seemed Gazali did not like Mujahid's abduction of school girls and their rape by Lakum-Hakum. Hardly would he finish preaching in his mosque without condemning the abduction and raping of girls. What Lakum-Hakum was doing was Satanic and unIslamic he kept preaching in his mosque. It is a fundamental rule of war in Islam that children and women were not to be harmed by belligerents. Not only should they not be harmed, they should be protected. For Mujahid, not only to abduct little girls but to rape them was to Gazali a heinous act he must condemn.

As Gazali got more virulent in his preaching against Lakum-Hakum, he received a surprised visit one afternoon by Dan'azumi who had broken away from Mujahid for the same reason. He was excited that Dan'azumi wanted to join ranks with him to fight Mujahid. Both Mujahid and Dan'azumi were his former pupils. One of the pupils has gone astray while the other wanted to join him to recover the lost one.

'When you see a hyena as a dove, it begins to look so; when you see a dove as a hyena, it begins to look so,' Gazali said while he and Dan'azumi sat lamenting Mujahid's jihad.

'I don't understand,' Dan'azumi said looking puzzled.

'Islam is a beast if you choose to see it as such; an angel if you choose to see it as such,' Gazali said.

'I see,' Dan'azumi said, the puzzle in his face dissolving into a genial smile.

'Jihad like everything in Islam has its rules,' Gazali said. 'It is not a blank cheque one can enter any amount. If it were so, Islam's bank of morality would have long been bankrupted.'

'That's true Mallam,' Dan'azumi said. 'What Mujahid is now doing is no longer on the path of Islam you taught us, but on the path of those that have gone astray. As far as I can see, what he is doing bears no relation with the path you set us on.'

'If what he is doing is Islam, then I wonder what is not Islam,' Gazali said.

'We have a historic responsibility to stop him or at least make the public, particularly the non-Moslem public, know what he is doing has nothing to do with Islam,' Dan'azumi said.

'Two sons; one is right, one is wrong. People should not blame the father too much,' Gazali said with a sardonic expression on his face.

'That's true Mallam,' Dan'azumi said. 'The chameleon has given birth to his children; whether they know how to dance or not is their problem.'

'That's also true,' Gazali said. 'Every tortoise carries its own shell.'

Dan'azumi did not say anything. He was wondering in his mind if Suleiman who he has always seen as something lame could be doing better for Islam with his jihad of the heart than they were with their jihad of the mouth and hand. Well, this was not something he could say to Gazali knowing the latter's position on the matter and the latter being his former teacher. So he said nothing.

If Gazali and Dan'azumi in preaching against Mujahid's insurgency wanted to make the latter less atrocious in his insurgency, they seemed not to be succeeding the way they wanted. Rather than toning down his insurgency, Mujahid seemed incensed by his teacher's and friend's preaching to be more vicious in his attacks. It was like he was spitting defiance at both his teacher and friend.

There was a saying among ancestral worshippers of Jeddere that when spirits are at war, the wind changes direction. If this saying was true, then the wind must have changed direction when Gazali clashed with his former pupil. Every week there were reports of various monstrous attacks by Lakum-Hakum. There was hardly any attack that less than fifty people were not killed.

Alongside the killings were abductions of secondary school girls. Because of lack of space to keep the girls, before a new set of girls were abducted, the one's earlier abducted were released after ascertaining they were pregnant by the insurgents' serial rapes.

If Gazali, Dan'azumi and Suleiman in going against Mujahid were trying to mobilize public opinion against Lakum-Hakum, they did not seem to be recording much success at least among pupils of madrasas who were mostly recruited for the jihad. Daily, more pupils trooped to Mujahid to be recruited for the holy war against infidels and so-called Moslems. Within four years of the commencement of the insurgency, Lakum-Hakum's various cells were bursting with insurgents.

While he waged his jihad, Mujahid's plot to kill Gazali, Dan'azumi, Suleiman and his father who had cursed him was thickening. 'To borrow from the rich repertoire of infidels' proverbs, true the sound of a gun does not rattle the gods, I am however the sound of the gun that rattles the gods,' he often said to himself. 'There is a difference between a chewing stick and the tail of a cobra. Mallam and Dan'azumi seem to be mistaking the tail of a cobra for a chewing stick. The rat that goes to meet the cobra in its hole does not live to tell the story. The two of you look to me like rats that are visiting the cobra in its hole. I am the porcupine no one marches without getting hurt.'

In a night he called *the night of the porcupine*, Mujahid killed Gazali his teacher, Dan'azumi and Suleiman his friends, but missed his father who seemed to have premonition of the assassination and fled. Not only did he kill Gazali, he killed his pupils for listening to his campaign against him.

He was very happy he killed Gazali his teacher. If his teacher's good ears could hear what was happening in hell, it was time he sent him there to see what he had been hearing.

Chapter Nineteen

While sad over his father escaping death in the night of the porcupine, Mujahid for weeks gloated over his success of killing Gazali, Dan'azumi and Suleiman. Killing the threesome truly proved he was the porcupine no one marches without getting hurt. With the threesome out of the way, the coast was clear for him to press on with his vision of Islam as a religion of war until everyone becomes a Moslem. There was no more fear of his vision being counteracted by the effeminate vision of peace while infidels and so-called Moslems held sway.

In his operational headquarters, Mujahid always had a harem of wives since he started abducting school girls. Of the various girls he had abducted and turned to wives, he loved Grace more than others and seemed more relaxed with her. He called her Gimbia to underscore his love for her. Girls that were abducted with Grace had since been released, but she was held behind by him.

The operational headquarters of Lakum-Hakum was divided into four quarters. There was a quarter for newly recruited insurgents, another for old insurgents, another for abducted girls, and another for Mujahid and his harem.

Grace lived with Mujahid in his quarters. Though a teenage girl, Grace was big and voluptuous. She was the type of woman Mujahid liked and that was part of the reason he was hooked to her. Apart from meeting his bodily taste in a woman, she had manners he found becoming and pleasing. She cooked well, cut his fingernails and took good care of his clothes. When he was around, she gave him all her attention.

Unknown to Mujahid, Grace's good manners were not heart-deep, but a show to lure him into being free with her. In her heart, she was seething with hate and anger. Mujahid had killed her father in an attack of her village by Lakum-Hakum. He had also raped her. How could she possibly love a man who had done these things to her if not for the folly of the man who thought so? Though Mujahid did not know he killed her father, he knew he raped her. Though he knew he raped her, he thought she was not angry with him because according to him she enjoyed the rape.

He never believed any woman for long could nurse bitter feelings against a man who raped her because she must have enjoyed the act as it progressed. Women he always said are pretentious creatures. Though a woman may not love a man, she is never genuinely offended if the man loves her. She may put up a show of offence when the man expresses his love for her, but inside she will be glowing with pride and happiness. Any man loving her is an additional testimonial of her worth. She deploys similar ambivalent attitude to rape. While affecting not to enjoy the act, she is most likely enjoying it more than the man raping her.

Below the surface, Grace was bidding the time she would strike to avenge her father's death and her rape. The time she was bidding came one Sunday Morning when the insurgents were observing their early morning prayer.

Mujahid had overslept perhaps because he was drunk the previous day. So he did not wake up to perform his morning prayers. Grace who used to wake him up if he overslept because he was drunk refused to wake him because she thought that day was the right day for her to exert vengeance. From his breathing, she knew he was in deep slumber. It was Sunday – a day she believed her God will deliver the philistine sleeping beside her to his own sword. She was the daughter of Zion and this fateful Sunday she believed the God of Joshua will make the walls of Jericho crumble before her feet without her shouting.

Moving quietly, she brought out Mujahid's sword which he had used to behead many people and beheaded him in one downward movement of the sword. There was no scream or violent movement of the body of the jihadist in the throes of death. His beheaded body only gave a few jerks before it lay still in death and his head only bounced once before it lay still beside the body of the insurgent. Grace thought it ironical that the body of a violent man like Mujahid was not violent in death.

Because Mujahid accepted Grace as a loyal abductee who would not be up to any mischief or attempt fleeing the camp, he did not look closely at whatever she was doing or monitor her movement in the camp. His followers observing his attitude towards her deployed the same attitude towards her. While they scrutinised the behaviour of other captives and monitor their movements, they neither scrutinized the behaviour of Grace nor monitored her movements.

When she beheaded Mujahid, Grace came out of the hut she and Mujahid slept and walked past the insurgents praying in the small mosque of the camp. One or two insurgents saw her while the remaining deeper in prayers did not.

As soon as she was out of their sight, Grace broke into a tearing run. She ran faster than her body build would ordinarily allow. At school, she was an athlete. It seemed her athletic skills were still with her despite many months of not being put to use.

Grace's fortune was that what she did was not discovered until about two hours later. By that time she was in a bus heading for her town.

The insurgents were used to Mujahid not appearing in the mosque to lead them in the early morning prayers. Whenever he did not do so, his assistant took his place. Used to him not appearing to lead them in morning prayers, they did not go to his tent on the fateful day of his murder to check on him. Most of them after their morning prayers went back to sleep. When around 7 am he was still not out of his tent, they thought this was unusual and went to his tent to find out why he had not come out of the tent that day only to find his beheaded body.